If flowers, trees and plants are to grow,
there must be spring storms and rain.

A storm releases itself,
as a human being must
when the mind is confused
and the heart is in pain
and the spirit is to be nourished.

CEREMONY — IN THE
CIRCLE OF LIFE

Story by
WHITE DEER OF AUTUMN

Illustrations by
DANIEL SAN SOUCI

BEYOND
WORDS
Publishing
I N C

There are four seasons in the complete circle of one year. Little Turtle has lived nine complete circles. He is a Native American boy growing up in the city. He knows little of the peace which comes from hearing the sounds of nature and seeing the beauty of the Earth. He knows even less of the wisdom and knowledge of his ancestors' beliefs.

Today, Little Turtle was hurt and lonely. When he missed his school bus, his classmates teased him for being late. They called him ''Slow Turtle.'' Even his teacher frowned at his long, windblown hair.

On his way home, Little Turtle decided to stop at his special place, a nearby city park. He knew that listening to the birds would make his heart feel lighter. But, arriving at the park, Little Turtle found giant earthmovers tearing up the land. His only true friends, the squirrels and the birds, were gone.

Now it is evening, and with the coming darkness, Little Turtle's sorrow deepens. Alone in his room, he begins to cry. He cannot understand the children at school making fun of him or his teacher being unfriendly. And now his special place is destroyed. Leaning on his windowsill, looking up at a group of stars flickering in the sky, Little Turtle cries out, ''Why? It's not fair!''

Suddenly, the boy is blinded by a brilliant light. Frightened, he backs away from the window as the light fills his room. Before his eyes, Little Turtle's walls become the Earth and Sky, and the light becomes an awesome figure, standing tall.

"Do not be afraid, Little Turtle. I am Star Spirit. I am from a long time past, yet I live today. I have traveled from the Seven Dancing Stars to teach you what many of Earth's people have forgotten. Listen, and you will remember!"

Star Spirit bends to the Earth and sifts the loose soil.

"Feel the Earth, Little Turtle. She is your cosmic mother. The elements of your body come from her and will return to her. Because she gives birth to all growing things and nourishes life, she deserves honor."

Little Turtle sadly remembers the big machines and the fallen trees in the park.

Star Spirit touches Little Turtle's shoulder. "I will show you how to comfort Mother Earth and soothe her with songs and ceremonies. You can honor her with the power of your words."

Star Spirit traces a circle at Little Turtle's feet and divides the shape into four equal parts. He fills each part with a different color of earth.

Little Turtle watches Star Spirit magically lift the circle from the ground.

''This is a symbol for the Circle of Life. Each color represents one of the Four Directions or a race of Man. They are not the same, but each shares an equal part of this Wheel of Life. Your ancestors thought of all life within the Circle as equal. Now, reach up, Little Turtle, and spin the sacred Wheel. Watch the colors mix and blend.''

''It's turning brown!'' the boy exclaims.

''Yes,'' Star Spirit says, ''the color of Mother Earth.''

When the Wheel stops spinning, Star Spirit lays it back on the ground. Like snow melting before the Sun, the Circle and its colors return to the Earth.

''The Circle is a sacred symbol for your Native People, Little Turtle. When they pray to the Four Directions, they form a circle. All their dances are danced in circles. I will teach you to keep the symbol of the Circle strong!''

Star Spirit motions upward, and a mist rises from the Earth to form a trail through the Sky. Together, he and Little Turtle reach the trail's end.

"See, Little Turtle, there is much more to the Circle of Life. Look down at Mother Earth. She is circular and round. And over there is your grandmother, the Moon. She travels in a circle across your father, the Sky."

Little Turtle squints at the great light of the Sun, and Star Spirit shields the boy's eyes.

"The Sun, a circle of fire, is your cosmic grandfather. All around us is the Universe, the great circle with no beginning and no end. Even the Stars above us are round. Your people call them the Path of Souls."

Little Turtle returns to Earth with Star Spirit. Excitedly, he says, "And I am round, too, like my Sky relatives!"

"Yes, Little Turtle, you and all the children of the Earth are circular and round. You are created in this way to live in harmony with the Earth and one another. Your animal and plant relatives also understand this. Listen now, Little Turtle, and they will tell you."

Little Turtle hears a twig snap and sees branches moving in the woods. A four-legged animal steps cautiously toward him.

''I am your older brother Deer. My antlers are pointed and sharp, but they are also circular and round. If there were no forest for me to live in, I would be easy prey for hunters.''

A voice gurgles from a pond at the edge of the clearing. Little Turtle crouches at the pool's edge to see who is there.

''I am Fish. Like the pond I live in, I am circular and round. I am happy living here, Little Turtle, but only because this water does not yet make me sick.''

Fish splashes beneath the surface of his home, and a sweet sound comes from the trees. Star Spirit carries Little Turtle swiftly through the air, high into the boughs of an ancient oak.

''I am Robin. See my nest? I built it in a circle. I am keeping the round eggs of my unborn babies warm.''

Little Turtle looks shyly into her nest.

Little Turtle glides with Star Spirit to the ground. He sees something moving in the meadow — moving closer to *him*. A long, thin creature rises from the grass.

"I am Snake, younger brother. Like the Earth I live close to, I am round."

Little Turtle is confused. "I think I am afraid of you."

"The world you live in has taught you to be afraid, Little Turtle. Long ago, many of your people had great respect for me. Some still do, for I am the protector of the Plant nations. With all the building and paving going on today, I am very worried."

Little Turtle forgets his fear of Snake as two delicate wings flutter around him. He hardly feels the insect land on his small arm. "Look, a butterfly!"

"No, Little Turtle, I am Luna Moth. Your world has not taught you the beauty of my nation. Look at the crescent moons on my wings."

As Luna Moth displays the markings on her pale wings, droplets of rain hit Little Turtle's outstretched arm.

A brief sunshower falls. Little Turtle watches in fascination as the rain turns everything around him into a garden of glistening colors.

The colors speak with one voice. "We are Flowers. Like growing things all over the Earth, we are circular and round.

"We have been blessed with rain. For this we are thankful. Look at the curved lines above us, Little Turtle. The Rainbow shows our thanks to the Creation. It is the Return of the Blessing."

Under the Rainbow, Star Spirit calls for all of Earth's children to join in a circle.

Little Turtle watches Star Spirit take a stone from the ground, then a branch from a small tree. Placing them together, they become a living Pipe.

To all, Star Spirit speaks. ''We have gathered in a circle with this sacred Pipe. I will fill it with tobacco. When we light the Pipe, we will talk to the Four Directions. This is our Ceremony.''

Star Spirit makes a sweeping motion over the Earth with the Pipe.

''Look at this land on which you live, the great Mother Earth. She is having a hard time taking care of her children! Proud trees are uprooted and cast aside to die. Animals are driven from their homes. The rivers which vein the Earth are filled with poison. Mother Earth needs to hear good and soothing sounds. Through the smoke from this Pipe, our words will become one with the air, and will touch all of nature.''

Star Spirit lights the Pipe and raises the stem to the East.

"You whose Power is the rising Sun, you are the birth and rebirth of life on this land. Your light is the symbol of knowledge and truth.

"Oh, Power of the rising Sun, shine your light into the hearts of Man, that he may understand the beauty of Mother Earth and let her be.

"Power of the rising Sun, you are life in its new beginning. Your season is Spring. Your color is Yellow."

Little Turtle watches Star Spirit smoke the Pipe.

When Star Spirit points the Pipe towards the South, a warm wind blows over the circle.

''You whose Power is the Sun high in the Sky, send your warm winds to carry seeds and pollen across this land, for they are the symbol of the promise for new life.

"Oh, Power of the Sun high in the Sky, warm the red blood flowing through the hearts of Man, that he may *feel* the beauty of Mother Earth and let her be.

"Power of the Sun high in the Sky, you are life in its prime. Your season is Summer. Your color is Red."

As Star Spirit turns to the West, darkness begins to cover the Sky. Little Turtle sees lightning flash from the gathering clouds.

"You whose Power is the setting Sun, you bring the night which reveals the Stars. Do not let the starlight go away from this land. It is the symbol of hope in Man's darkness of fear and ignorance, hate and war.

"Oh, Power of the setting Sun, send the thunder and rain to cleanse the Earth and make her pure again. Make your Thunderers *shake* the bones of Man, that he may see the beauty of Mother Earth and let her be.

"Power of the setting Sun, you are life in its maturity. Your season is Autumn. Your color is Black."

Star Spirit sends his words skyward, and the darkness fades.

Little Turtle feels snowflakes fall wet and cold on his cheek as Star Spirit addresses the North.

"You whose Power is the distant Sun, the snow you send is the white blanket covering much of this land. It is the symbol of purity in the words we speak and the life we live.

"Oh, Power of the distant Sun, send your winds to cool the fevered hearts of Man that he may know the beauty of Mother Earth and let her be.

"Power of the distant Sun, you are life at its ending and great change. Your season is Winter. Your color is White."

After heart-sent words to both Father Sky and Mother Earth, Star Spirit lifts the Pipe.

> Holding you, sacred Pipe, with gentle
> firmness, I reach my arms high.
> You, like lightning from the Thunder Beings,
> are a link between Earth and Sky.

Little Turtle listens carefully as Star Spirit passes the Pipe over the Circle of Life.

''Great Mystery, Source of Life, Your presence is in all Creation, for You are the life of Creation.

''We are tiny parts of life in Your vast Universe. This makes us feel small, and not so important at all. Yet we are part of You.

''This awareness makes our hearts soar!

''Great Mystery, if Man is to live in harmony with the Earth, he needs the peace which comes from realizing that he shares life with all Creation. He must know that the power to keep things beautiful is Your power in all people.

''Oh, may the Circle live!''

In the silence of the Circle, Star Spirit's words become puffs of smoke. A soft breeze lifts them into the Sky.

Looking about, Little Turtle sees the flowers and animals begin to disappear. Once again, he is in his bedroom. Only Star Spirit remains, near the open window.

"For now, Little Turtle, it is done. I have given you another special place, the world of your Vision. It cannot be destroyed.

"Take this living Pipe, protect it, and use it as I have. Live with new strength, Little Turtle, and remember this: All things are part of the great Circle of Life, and all over the Universe are your relatives. *You are never alone.*"

The image of Star Spirit begins to fade as the fire in the Pipe grows brighter.

"I am leaving now, but you can always find me in the light of a distant Star, or in the spark glowing nearest your heart."

Little Turtle receives the Pipe and holds it close.

This book was written in keeping with my Vision.

It is for the people of good heart, that they may share it with their children.

The colors of the Four Directions and their location in the Wheel of Life vary somewhat from tribe to tribe. I chose this special symbol because of its universal appeal for Native American people.

The beauty of my home in the Land of Flowers (Florida), the destruction inflicted on Her by Civilized Man, and the love I bear our Native children created the purpose and the need for *Ceremony—In the Circle of Life*.

— *White Deer of Autumn*

Gabriel Horn was named "White Deer" by Princess Red Wing of the Narraganset Tribe-Wampanoag Nation, and was educated in the traditional concepts of his People by Nippawanock and Metacomet, his uncles. White Deer of Autumn is former Cultural Arts Director of the Minneapolis American Indian Center and he currently devotes much of his time to lecturing and teaching. White Deer and his Ojibwa wife Simone ("Loon Song") live in St. Petersburg, Florida with their three children Ihasha, Calusa, and Carisis. This is his first book for children, but White Deer's poetry has appeared in numerous quarterlies and anthologies. The author dedicates this book "to my uncles, Nippawanock and Metacomet."

Other Native American Titles by Gabriel Horn: *The Great Change* ($13.95 hardcover, ages 5-12). A wise grandmother explains the meaning of death, or the Great Change, to her questioning granddaughter. It is a moving tale for everyone who wonders about what lies beyond this life. Watercolor illustrations by internationally acclaimed painter, Carol Grigg. *Native People, Native Ways Series* ($4.95 per volume, softcover, ages 10-14). The four books in this series are designed around the Native American Circle of Life. "The Book of Knowledge," "The Book of Life," "The Book of Change," and "The Book of Wisdom" all explore the history, culture, traditions, myths, contributions, and challenges of the Native American peoples. The Native American story, as told by a Native American.

Daniel San Souci was born in California and graduated from the California College of Arts and Crafts. His paintings have won numerous awards, and his work is on display in various galleries and in private collections. He has created the illustrations for three children's books, *The Brave Little Tailor, Song of Sedna,* and *The Legend of Scarface,* which was chosen as one of the "Best Illustrated Children's Books of 1978" by *The New York Times*.

Mr. San Souci lives in Oakland, California, with his wife and their two children Yvette and Justin. The artists dedicates this book "to my wife Loretta."